Dolphin Dreaming

Story by Jan Weeks
Illustrations by Meredith Thomas

Harcourt Achieve
Rigby • Steck-Vaughn

www.HarcourtAchieve.com
1.800.531.5015

PM Extras Chapter Books
Emerald

U.S. Edition © 2006 Harcourt Achieve Inc.
10801 N. MoPac Expressway
Building #3
Austin, TX 78759
www.harcourtachieve.com

Text © 2003 Cengage Learning Australia Pty Limited
Illustrations © 2003 Cengage Learning Australia Pty Limited
Originally published in Australia by Cengage Learning Australia

All rights reserved. No part of the material protected by this copyright may be reproduced or utilized in any form or by any means, in whole or in part, without permission in writing from the copyright owner. Requests for permission should be mailed to: Copyright Permissions, Harcourt Achieve Inc., P.O. Box 27010, Austin, Texas 78755.

Rigby and Steck-Vaughn are trademarks of Harcourt Achieve Inc. registered in the United States of America and/or other jurisdictions.

2 3 4 5 6 7 8   1957   14 13 12 11 10
4500206462

Text: Jan Weeks
Printed in China by 1010 Printing International Ltd

Dolphin Dreaming
ISBN 978 0 75 789360 5

Contents

CHAPTER 1
Mermaid Point — 4

CHAPTER 2
The Ledge — 10

CHAPTER 3
The Other Side — 15

CHAPTER 4
Dolphins — 20

CHAPTER 5
I Did It! — 26

CHAPTER 1

Mermaid Point

When Dad had to go overseas, he asked my grandparents if Jess and I could stay with them. Mom died when I was a baby, and Dad's job takes him away a lot. We spend lots of time with Grandma and Grandpa Ellis. Dad often asks them to look after us. It's an easy solution to the problem.

Mermaid Point

Not that we're ever any trouble. We love staying with our grandparents and they like having us. Mom had been their only child, and we're the only family they have left.

This time our stay was going to be different. Grandma and Grandpa Ellis had decided to rent a house for the summer in a little town on the south coast. It was called Mermaid Point. Jess and I had never been there, but even its name stirred our imaginations. Our heads were filled with pictures of white sand, sparkling blue water, and ships passing by far out to sea.

"It's going to be so much fun, Tegan," Jess said as she hugged me. "We'll be able to go swimming every day. And we'll get to ride the body boards Dad bought us as a going away present. Won't that be fantastic?"

"Great," I answered, not feeling quite so confident. Jess is two years older than me. She isn't afraid of anything, even though she was born hearing impaired and needs to wear a hearing aid. She can read lips and doesn't let her handicap bother her—most of the time. I was doing my best to be brave like her, but it wasn't easy.

There was a railway station in a town not far from Mermaid Point. Grandma and Grandpa Ellis had arranged to meet us there. It was the first time Jess and I had traveled such a long way by train, and we loved it. I sat facing her so we could talk. It made us feel grown up to know that Dad trusted us enough to let us make the trip by ourselves.

As we drew near the station, I began to wonder if it had been such a good idea. "What are we going to do if they are not there to meet us, Jess?" I asked. "What will we do then?"

"You have to stop worrying about everything, Tegan," Jess answered. "They'll be there."

And Jess was right. As the train pulled in, I could see Grandma and Grandpa Ellis standing on the platform, waving to us.

"I told you there was no need to worry," Jess said.

CHAPTER 2

The Ledge

The house my grandparents had rented was on a hill. From the front porch, we could look out over the ocean and see the huge rocks that formed Mermaid Point. The point extended quite a ways under the water separating the sea into two bays. Each bay had its own beach.

We swam at the beach in front of my grandparents' house. To get to the other beach, we would have to climb up the rocks to the path that led along a ledge and then climb down the rocks on the other side of the point.

We had only been at Mermaid Point two days when Jess said she wanted to explore the second beach.

"It'll be fun," she said, grabbing my arm. "How will we know what's there unless we go and see for ourselves?"

As I looked at the ledge, I wondered if I really wanted to know. The ledge was high and it didn't look very wide. "Why don't we go for a swim instead and leave the exploring for another day?" I suggested.

"We've already been in the water many times," Jess answered. "Come on, Tegan! It isn't dangerous. People walk along the ledge all the time. Why else would there be a path?"

Without waiting for an answer, Jess ran ahead, looking like a mountain goat as she scampered over the rocks. I followed, using my hands to steady myself as I moved gingerly from rock to rock.

Getting to the ledge was the easy part. As I looked up at my sister, I wondered if she could hear the waves crashing below.

The Ledge

The wind was whipping her hair, and she laughed as she held out her hand to help me onto the ledge. The path was over a yard wide and cut into the side of a cliff. Tree roots, moss, and patches of grass bordered the edge closest to the cliff. On the other side of the path there was a sheer drop.

"Try not to look down," Jess said.

She was too late. I had already done that. Far below me I could now see the waves I had heard before splashing against the jagged rocks, covering everything in white swirling foam. It made my stomach lurch and I felt dizzy. I stood like a statue, frozen with fear.

"Don't be such a scaredy cat, Tegan!" Jess said, turning back to face me. She was already half way across the ledge.

"I can't do it," I answered, as I pushed my back into the side of the cliff. "I'm going back."

"Suit yourself," Jess said, as she shrugged her shoulders. "You're the one who is going to miss out. Not me!"

I didn't care. I only knew I had to get off the ledge before I fell off it.

CHAPTER 3
The Other Side

I waited on the beach for Jess. She was gone a long time. When she came back, she couldn't stop talking about the bay on the other side of Mermaid Point.

"You'll never guess what I saw while I was over there," she said. "There was a mother dolphin and her baby swimming in the water. You should have come with me, Tegan. You would have loved them."

Dolphins are my favorite animals. Dad took us to a theme park last year, and we saw them doing tricks. I thought then how wonderful it would be to swim with them.

The mother and baby playing in the water on the other side of Mermaid Point were almost enough to make me wish I had gone with Jess, but when I thought of how afraid I'd been on the ledge, I shivered and quickly changed my mind.

Mr. Gray was at our house when we got home. He was an old friend of Grandpa's and had moved to Mermaid Point to live after he'd retired. Mr. Gray had been the one who suggested my grandparents rent the house.

The Other Side

When Jess told Mr. Gray she'd seen dolphins in the bay, he answered that he'd seen them that morning as well. Mr. Gray loved fishing and had gone there to throw in his line.

"I think I counted eight of them this morning," he said.

"I only saw a mother and a baby when I was there," Jess answered. "The rest must have swum back out to sea."

"Isn't it dangerous walking along the ledge?" Grandma asked. She didn't want anything to happen to us, especially when she was looking after us.

"Fishermen use the path all the time," Mr. Gray answered. "The girls will be safe enough, as long as they keep away from the edge."

"Jess and Tegan aren't likely to do anything silly," Grandpa assured Grandma. He thinks we're both very responsible for our age.

"You're right, of course," Grandma answered, as she smiled at me.

I'm not the one she should be worrying about, I thought. Jess is the daredevil of the family.

"I can hardly wait to see the dolphins again," Jess said that night, as we were getting ready for bed. "We'll go tomorrow morning after breakfast."

"Is there any other way to get there?" I asked, thinking of the ledge and the rocks below it.

"Only if you're a seagull," Jess laughed. "There's no need for you to be frightened, Tegan. You won't fall. I'll help you."

CHAPTER 4

Dolphins

That night I dreamt I was swimming with the dolphins. I held out my hand to touch them as they swam around me, playing with me, butting my body with their funny noses, doing acrobatics in the water. It was like I was in a different world, a world so amazing I didn't want to wake up.

When I did, I knew I had to go to the bay to see them. Nobody knew how long the mother and her baby would be there. They could be gone already, and I would have missed my opportunity.

The first thing I heard as I sat up in bed was Jess sneezing. Then she began to cough. "We'll have to put off going to the bay for another day," she said. "My head hurts and I feel really sick. I think I'm getting a cold."

Jess has to be careful because a cold could cause ear infections, which really bother her. My grandparents suggested she stay in bed, and Jess didn't argue.

Dolphins

So I told Grandma and Grandpa that I was going to the beach by myself. I sat drawing a dolphin in the sand with a stick and thought about crossing the ledge on my own. I tried to muster up the courage to do it.

Finally I made up my mind. If I wanted to see the dolphins, I was going to have to cross the ledge by myself.

Dolphin Dreaming

Dolphins

Once again, climbing the rocks was the easy part. Walking along the ledge was a different story. At least this time the waves were quiet below.

"Don't look down," I told myself. "Look straight ahead. Pretend you're walking in the park." It was easy to say, but much harder to do.

Step by nervous step, I inched my way across the ledge until at last I was on the other side.

"There now!" I said to myself. "That wasn't so bad, was it?" But I was already dreading the thought of going back.

The dolphins were still there. Only now there were eight of them. Mr. Gray's dolphins had come back. They were swimming in pairs, leaping in the air, then plunging back into the water, only to resurface a few moments later. One had a fish in its mouth. It was tossing it into the air, playing with it. Another swam almost to the beach, before diving under the waves and swimming out into the bay again.

Dolphins

I was so absorbed in their play, I forgot about the ledge. All I could think of was the dolphins. I longed to jump into the water to swim with them, as I had in my dream, but I'm not a strong swimmer, and I was alone. So I sat on a rock, content just to watch them.

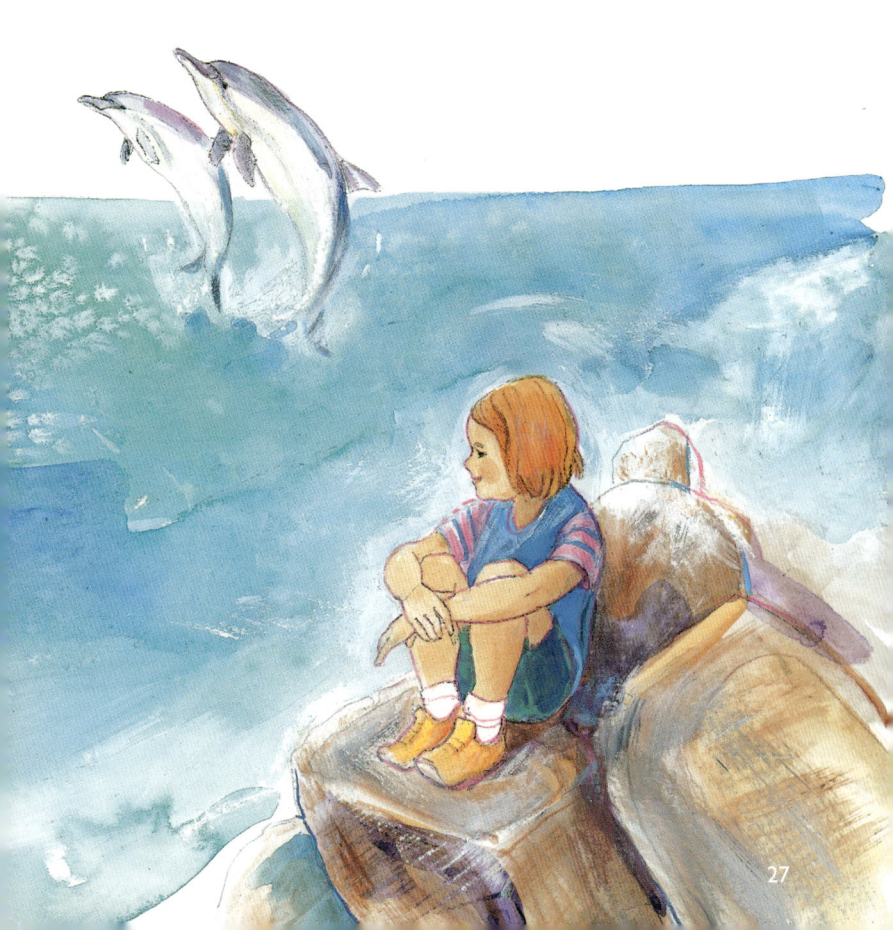

CHAPTER 5
I Did It!

Before I knew it, hours had gone by. The sun was more than halfway across the sky. It was past lunchtime. Grandma and Grandpa would be wondering where I was.

"I'd better hurry," I told myself as I began to climb up to the ledge.

The wind had changed and now I could hear the waves splashing onto the rocks. I could see them below me, waiting for me to fall.

"I can't do it!" I yelled as I pushed my back into the cliff. "I'm too scared!"

Nobody heard me, except for some gulls flying overhead, and they didn't care whether I fell or not. "Don't be such a baby!" I told myself. "You have to go back. Grandma and Grandpa will be worried about you."

Dolphin Dreaming

With my back pressed against the cliff and my heart pounding, I took a small step sideways.

Realizing I wasn't going to fall, I took another step and then another, until at last I reached the rocks on the other side of the ledge. Then all I had to do was climb down to the sand.

Grandma and Grandpa were waiting for me on the beach. They looked pleased to see me. "Jess said you'd be too scared to walk across the ledge," they told me.

"I was scared," I answered. "But I had to see the dolphins before they swam back out to sea."

Jess was sitting in the kitchen when we went back to the house.

"It was brave of you to walk along the ledge on your own," she said. "I'm proud of you, Tegan. You didn't let your fears stop you from doing something that you really wanted to do."

"It was the dolphins that made me brave," I answered. "Without them, I would never have found the courage. Do you want to know something else, Jess? They were worth every minute of it. They were amazing!"